Welcome to
Hopscotch Hill School!
In Miss Sparks's class,
you will make friends
with children just like you.
They love school,
and they love to learn!
Keep an eye out for Razzi,
the class pet rabbit.
He may be anywhere!
See if you can spot him
as you read the story.

Welcome!

Students of the Week!

Miss Sparks

Logan

Connor

Hallie

Gwen

Avery

Spencer

Nathan

Razzi

Skylar

Delaney

Lindy

Published by Pleasant Company Publications
Copyright © 2005 by American Girl, LLC
All rights reserved. No part of this book may be used or reproduced
in any manner whatsoever without written permission except in the case
of brief quotations embodied in critical articles and reviews.
For information, address:
Book Editor, Pleasant Company Publications, 8400 Fairway Place,
P.O. Box 620998, Middleton, WI 53562.

Visit our Web site at **americangirl.com**.

Printed in China
05 06 07 08 09 10 C&C 10 9 8 7 6 5 4 3 2 1

Hopscotch Hill School™ and logo,
Where a love for learning grows™, Logan™, and
American Girl® are trademarks of American Girl, LLC.

Cataloging-in-Publication data available from the Library of Congress

The Fair-Share Pair

by Valerie Tripp *illustrated by* Renate Lohmann

It's Pajama Day! Hurray!

It was a rainy day.

But the children in

Miss Sparks's classroom

were happy and wiggly and giggly.

Miss Sparks said, "Today we are

going to talk about

same and **different.**

How is today different

from yesterday?"

The children shouted,

"It's pajama day! Hurray!"

Miss Sparks smiled.

She said, "Who can use the words

same and **different**

to talk about pajama day?"

Hallie said, "Today we look the same because we are all wearing pajamas. But our pajamas look different because we like different things."

Skylar said, "I have stars on my pajamas.

Gwen has soccer balls.

Nathan has a superhero.

Connor has cars.

And Logan has flowers."

Miss Sparks said, "Yes!

I hope that

we can go outside soon

and see flowers

like the ones on Logan's pajamas."

All the children said, "We do too!"

But when it was time for recess,

it was still raining.

The children had to stay inside.

Connor and Logan played
in the toy corner.
Connor played with two cars.
Logan used blocks to make an arch.
Connor said, "That looks like a bridge."
Logan said, "I am pretending
that it is a rainbow.

But you can pretend

that it is a bridge.

We can share it.

We will be the fair-share pair."

"Thanks, Logan," said Connor.

"Would you like to use the red car?

You can pretend that it can

fly over the rainbow."

"Thanks!" said Logan.

Connor and Logan had fun

sharing the cars and the blocks.

Miss Sparks said, "Look, children!

The sun is shining at last!

Let's go outside."

The children rushed to

put on their coats and boots.

Logan was first to line up by the door.

Connor was last because

he stopped to get the cars

from the toy corner.

Miss Sparks led the children outside.

They ran and jumped and twirled.

They were so glad to

be outside!

Logan ran to the edge

of the blacktop.

She knelt down next to a

big, beautiful mud puddle.

There was a rainbow in it!

There were twigs and pebbles

and wiggly worms

in it too.

Connor knelt down by Logan.

He faced the blacktop

instead of the puddle.

Connor liked the way the rain

had washed the blacktop clean.

It was shiny and slick.

It looked like a racetrack.

Connor raced the red car

and the blue car

on the blacktop.

Vroom! Zoom!

Sometimes the red car won.

Sometimes the blue car won.

Just then Logan said, "Look, Connor!

There's a ladybug

in this puddle!"

Connor said, "The puddle must look
like a lake to the ladybug."
Logan said, "You just gave me
a great idea.
I will make Ladybug Land.
It will be a tiny land just
perfect for ladybugs to live in."
Logan pushed up her sleeves
and went to work.
She scooped up mud to make houses.
She lined up pebbles to make roads.

She put leaves in the puddle

to make boats.

Logan liked making Ladybug Land

in the muddy puddle.

Connor liked racing the cars

on the clean, shiny blacktop.

Logan said to Connor,

"We are playing different games.

But we feel the same.

We both feel happy!"

A Muddy, Mucky Mess

Logan asked, "Hey, Connor,
may I use the red car again?
It's perfect for my Ladybug Land.
I can pretend it is a
flying Ladybug Bus."
Connor looked at
Logan's muddy hands.
He did not want the
red car to get dirty.
But Connor knew
that Miss Sparks's
number one class rule
was, "We take turns."
So even though he did not want to,
Connor gave the red car to Logan.
"Thanks!" said Logan.

Connor ran the blue car

along the blacktop.

But he could not have races

with only one car.

He looked over his shoulder

to see what Logan was doing.

Logan was pretending

the red car was flying.

Then *splash!*

She landed the red car

in the puddle.

She drove the red car

straight through the mud.

She drizzled muddy water on it.

She buried it under

a lump of mud and left it there.

Connor thought that was

a terrible way to treat the red car.

He said, "May I have

the red car back now?"

"Sure," said Logan.

She dug the red car

out of the mud.

She held it out

to Connor.

Connor took it

with his fingertips.

The red car was a muddy, mucky mess!

It looked more brown than red.

The wheels were so muddy

that they would not turn.

The windshield was muddy too.

Connor frowned.

Logan said, "What's the matter?"

Connor said, "You got the car so dirty."

Logan said, "Oh! Sorry!

I was just having fun with it.

Give it back to me. I will clean it."

Connor gave Logan the red car.

Logan swooped the car

through the puddle.

Then she wiped it off on her pants

and gave it back to Connor.

A Muddy, Mucky Mess

Logan said, "There you go. All better."

But the car still looked

terrible to Connor.

He tried to clean it with a tissue.

But it was still streaked with mud.

Logan said, "Gosh, Connor!

A little mud never hurt anything.

I think you are too fussy."

Connor said, "I think YOU

are too messy."

When recess was over
the children went inside.
Connor parked the blue car
and the red car on his desk.
Miss Sparks said,
"Connor, please use the words
same and **different** to tell us
about the cars on your desk."
Connor said, "They were the
same when I played with them.

They were both clean.

Then Logan got mud on the red car.

Now the cars are different.

One is clean and one is dirty."

Miss Sparks said,

"Logan likes mud.

You do not.

Sometimes two people

have different feelings

about the same thing."

Connor looked at Logan.

She was smiling.

Logan did not seem to care that

she had made the red car

a muddy, mucky mess!

Right then Connor

made up his mind.

He would not share the red car

with Logan again.

He hid both cars in his desk

so Logan could not find them.

The next day Miss Sparks said,

"Children, you may go

outside for recess.

Put on your coats and boots."

Connor went to his cubby

to get his coat

and his boots.

He saw Logan go

to the toy corner

and look and look

for the red car.

Connor hurried to his desk.

He slipped the cars

into his coat pocket.

Connor was first to line up

by the door.

Logan was last to line up because

she had looked so long for the cars.

Connor knew he was not being fair

about sharing the red car.

But then he remembered how

Logan had gotten the red car so dirty.

Connor was sure he did NOT

want to share the red car with Logan

EVER AGAIN.

Squirt! Splash! Rub-a-dub!

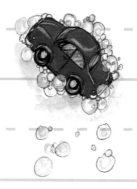

Miss Sparks led the class outside.

Logan and Hallie knelt

next to Ladybug Land.

Connor went to a different part

of the blacktop.

He raced the blue car and the red car.

Vroom! Zoom!

Suddenly Connor heard

someone say, "Hey!"

Connor looked up and saw Logan.

Logan put her hands

on her hips.

She said, "I looked all over

for that red car.

I want to show Hallie

how I play with it."

29

Logan picked up the red car.

"Please put that down," said Connor.

Logan hid the red car behind her back.

She said, "You have the blue car.

You don't need two cars."

"Yes, I do," said Connor.

"I'm racing them."

"That's not fair," said Logan.

"You have to share."

Connor said, "I shared

the red car with you yesterday.

You were not careful with it.

You got it all muddy."

Logan said, "The red car

does not belong to you.

I can play with it any way I want."

Logan ran back to Ladybug Land.

Connor followed her.

"Give me that red car!" Connor said.

"No!" said Logan.

Connor felt his face get hot.

He tried to take the

red car out of Logan's hand.

The red car fell in the mud puddle.

Kerplop!

Connor lifted

the red car

out of the puddle

with his fingertips.

Mud dripped from it.

"You did it again!" said Connor angrily.

"You got the red car all muddy."

"I did NOT," said Logan. "YOU did."

Logan stamped her foot in the puddle.

Splash!

Mud splashed up on Logan.

Mud splashed up on Connor

and the two cars too.

Miss Sparks rushed over.

The sparkles on her eyeglasses

were not glittering at all.

Miss Sparks said, "Connor and Logan!

What's the matter?"

Logan said, "It's not fair.

Connor won't share the red car."

Miss Sparks asked,

"Is that true, Connor?"

Connor's face got red.

Connor said, "I am sorry, Miss Sparks.

But Logan gets the red car too dirty."

Logan said, "We can't share because

we are too different.

I am fun. He is fussy."

"I like things clean," said Connor.

"She likes things messy."

"Children," said Miss Sparks,

"you are different in some ways.

But you are the same

in some ways too.

Right now you are both muddy.

Go inside and wash up.

And try to think

of a fair way

to share the cars."

Connor felt sorry

about the fight with Logan.

Logan felt sorry too.

But neither one could think

of a way to make things better.

Connor and Logan went inside.

They went to the sink.

Connor squirted soap on his hands.

Logan squirted soap on her hands.

Connor turned on the water.

They washed the mud off themselves.

Then Connor squirted soap on the cars.

He held the cars under

the stream of water.

Soon they were covered with

lots of lovely bubbles.

Logan said, "The cars look

like they are at the car wash."

Connor said, "That's a great idea.

Let's pretend the sink is a car wash."

Logan said, "Okay! That will be fun."

Squish, squirt!

Connor and Logan squirted soap
on the cars.

Splish, splash!

They drove the cars through the
stream of water.

Rub-a-dub-dub!

They rubbed the cars dry.

Squish, squirt!
Splish, splash!
Rub-a-dub-dub!
Connor and Logan
sent the cars through the
car wash again and again.
When Miss Sparks came
inside, the sparkles on
her eyeglasses glittered.
"I knew you two
could find a way to share.
You are different.
But you are the same
in one important way.
You each have a good imagination!"

Connor and Logan smiled.

Then Connor said to Logan,

"I know how we can both

have our fair share

of playing with the red car."

Logan asked, "How?"

Connor said, "Some days you

can play with it in Ladybug Land.

Some days I will race it.

But every day we can share it

by playing car wash together."

Logan said, "Okay.

That way we'll really be

the fair-share pair!"

Dear Parents . . .

Just as Connor did, your child knows that house rules—and class rules—call for sharing. But knowing that she *should* share is different from knowing *how* to share. Your child is still learning how to take turns in a way that's fair for all her friends. She's discovering that sometimes it's okay *not* to share. And she's realizing that sharing is a two-way street. She needs to take good care of things that she borrows just as she hopes her friends will take good care of the special things she shares with them.

You can give your child some strategies that will make it more fun for her to share, take turns, and compromise with others. You can encourage her to show respect for other people's things, as well as for her own. And you can help her learn the most valuable lesson of all—that most things really *are* more fun when they're shared with friends!

Fair Sharing

Your child knows that she should usually be generous and share, but does she know when it's okay *not* to share? Help her set her own personal rules for sharing. With a few boundaries, she'll feel more generous—and less anxious—about offering her things to friends.

• Talk with your child about the things that we just don't share. We don't share toothbrushes, combs, or hats, and it's okay not to share extra-special possessions either. Give your child a basket or box that she can use to **tuck away a few special toys** before friends come over. Make a deal that she will share the *rest* of the toys in her bedroom, playroom, or backyard.

- When you and your child check out library books, ask the librarian what rules the library has for borrowing items. Is there a time limit? A fine for damaged books? Let your child know that when she shares, **she can have one or two rules** of her own. It's okay to let a friend know that certain toys can only be played with inside or that the friend shouldn't eat a messy snack while she's reading a borrowed book.

- Reread page 17 of *The Fair-Share Pair*. Ask your child how she thinks Connor feels when Logan wants to borrow the red car. Talk about how sharing can lead to two different feelings—good, friendly feelings and anxious feelings, too. Tell your child that it's okay to have **mixed-up feelings** about sharing. That's why you are proud of her when she finds good ways to share.

- Help your child **focus on those good feelings** that come from sharing. Invite her along when you take flowers to a neighbor or clothes to a shelter. Do family activities that encourage sharing, such as jigsaw puzzles that require everyone to work toward a common goal. Share some of your dessert with your child, and thank her when she offers some of hers to you, too!

It's Your Turn!

Your child can decide what she wants to share at home, but sharing in the classroom is a different story. There, your child needs to take turns with classroom toys and to compromise when she and a friend want to play with the same toy in different ways. How can you help?

• Practice taking turns at home. At dinner, pass a flashlight around the table. Whoever holds the flashlight is **in the spotlight** and can share a story from her day. Take turns with special privileges, too, such as choosing a game for the family to play or deciding what to have for dessert. Let one family member be **Chooser** on Mondays, another on Tuesdays, and so forth throughout the week so that everyone has a fair share of turns.

Dear Parents . . .

- Reread pages 20 and 21 of *The Fair-Share Pair*, where Connor and Logan call each other "fussy" and "messy." Ask your child how she thinks Connor feels about the muddy car, and then ask how Logan feels about it. Ask, "Can **two people have different feelings** about the same thing?" Help your child come up with examples of things that she and a friend feel differently about. Emphasize that people can have different feelings and *still* be friends.

- Before a play date, play a **"what if . . ." game** and brainstorm ways to resolve conflicts. Ask your child, "What if there aren't enough toys for everyone to have her own to play with?" Could the children use a timer to give each friend a fair share of time with a toy? What if friends want to play different games at the same time? Can they play one game for 15 minutes and then move on to the next game?

- After teaching your child new sharing strategies, give her the power to use them. If she and a friend have trouble sharing, say, "Can you each think of two ways to share that toy?" If they can resolve their dispute, praise them for using their imaginations and finding a way to **play fairly and have fun**.

Borrowing Basics

When Logan returned the red car to Connor, it was a muddy, mucky mess! Carefree Logan broke one of the rules of borrowing, which is that when you borrow something, you must return it in good condition. You can teach your child some borrowing basics so that she'll learn to be responsible with other people's things, as well as with her own.

• Dedicate space in your child's room for storing books that she borrows from the library. Is it an empty shelf in her bookcase? A canvas book bag that hangs on her doorknob? Help her write and **decorate a list of rules** for caring for those books, such as "Don't bend the pages" and "Return books on time." Reward the special care she gives the books with a bookmark or a trip back to the library for more.

- Ask neighbors and friends in your area if they would like to **start a toy co-op.** Sort through your child's toys to help her choose those that she no longer plays with but that are in good condition. Donate those to the co-op, and let your child "check out" toys donated by others. Borrowing and lending toys will give her practice caring for things, and it'll reduce the clutter in her bedroom, too!

- When your child visits a friend, ask her if she'd like to **take a toy to share.** Toting along something of her own will remind her of the rules of borrowing: Ask first. Use the toy carefully. Give the toy back when you are done.

- Oh, dear! Accidents happen, and sometimes borrowed toys are damaged, broken beyond repair, or even lost forever. Help your child find the right way to **apologize to a friend for the loss of a toy.** Could she write the friend a note, or draw a picture, or offer a toy of her own as a replacement? Encourage your child to **be forgiving** when one of her toys or books is damaged or lost. Remind her that friends are always more important than things!

This story and the "Dear Parents" activities were developed with guidance from the Hopscotch Hill School advisory board.

Dominic Gullo is a professor of Early Childhood Education at Queens College, City University of New York. He is a member of the governing board of the National Association for the Education of Young Children, and he is a consultant to school districts across the country in the areas of early childhood education, curriculum, and assessment.

Margaret Jensen has taught beginning reading for 32 years and is currently a math resource teacher in the Madison Metropolitan School District, Wisconsin. She has served on committees for the International Reading Association and the Wisconsin State Reading Association, and has been president of the Madison Area Reading Council. She has presented at workshops and conferences in the areas of reading, writing, and children's literature.

Kim Miller is a school psychologist at Stephens Elementary in Madison, Wisconsin, where she works with children, parents, and teachers to help solve—and prevent—problems related to learning and adjustment to the classroom setting.

Virginia Pickerell has worked with teachers and parents as an educational consultant and counselor within the Madison Metropolitan School District. She has researched and presented workshops on topics such as learning processes, problem solving, and creativity. She is also a former director of Head Start.